CAN YOU FIND THESE ITEMS IN THE STORY?

Happy Birthday, Little Hoo!

Brenda Ponnay

On Monday, Little Hoo asked, "Is today my birthday?"

"Not today, Little Hoo," said Mama Hoo. "TEN more days until your birthday."

On Tuesday, Little Hoo asked, "Is today my birthday?"

"Not today, Little Hoo."
"Today is Market Day.

"NINE more days until your birthday."

On Wednesday, Little Hoo asked, "Is today my birthday?"

"No, Little Hoo. Today we go to the piñata store."

EIGHT more days
until your birthday.

On Thursday, Little Hoo asked,
"Is today my birthday?"

"No, Little Hoo.
Today is Mail Day.

SEVEN more days
until your birthday!"

On Friday, Little Hoo asked, "Is today my birthday?"

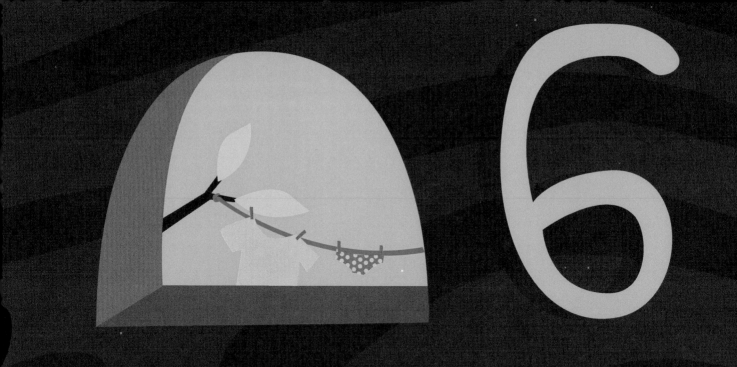

"No, Little Hoo.
Today is Laundry Day.

SIX more days until your birthday!"

On Saturday,
Little Hoo asked,
"Is today my birthday?"

"No, Little Hoo.
Today is Help-Your-Dad-
in-the-Yard Day.

FIVE more days
until your
birthday."

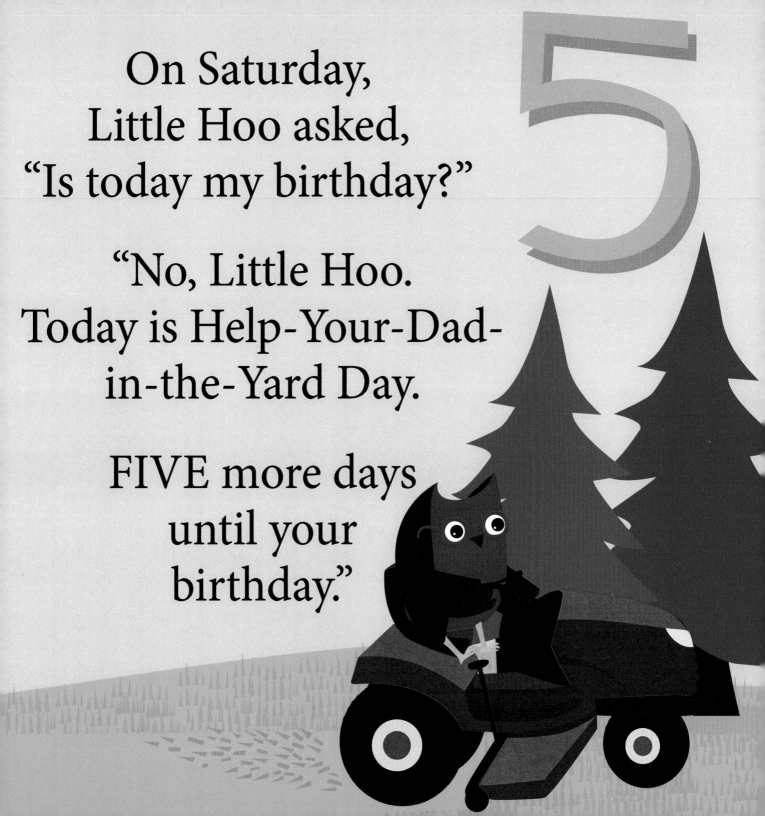

On Sunday, Little Hoo asked, "Is today my birthday?"

"No, Little Hoo. Today we are going to the candy store.

FOUR more days until your birthday!"

PARTY GAMES
Knock Knock Moo Who?
{and other silly animal jokes}
Brenda Ponnay

On Monday,
Little Hoo asked,
"Is today my birthday?"

"No, Little Hoo.
Today is Library Day.
THREE more days
until your birthday."

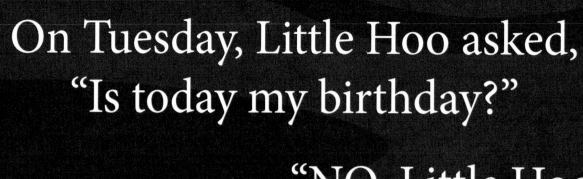

On Tuesday, Little Hoo asked, "Is today my birthday?"

"NO, Little Hoo. Today is Clean-the-House Day

and Bake-a-Cake Day!

2

TWO more days until your birthday!"

On Wednesday, Little Hoo asked, "Is today my birthday?"

"NO, Little Hoo. Today is Decorate-the-House and Ice-the-Cake Day!

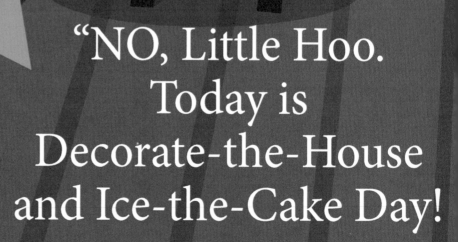

ONE more day
until your birthday!"

On Thursday, Little Hoo asked, "Is today my birthday?"

LET'S PARTY!

MAKE YOUR OWN LITTLE HOO PARTY GAME!

CUT ALONG THE DOTTED LINES.

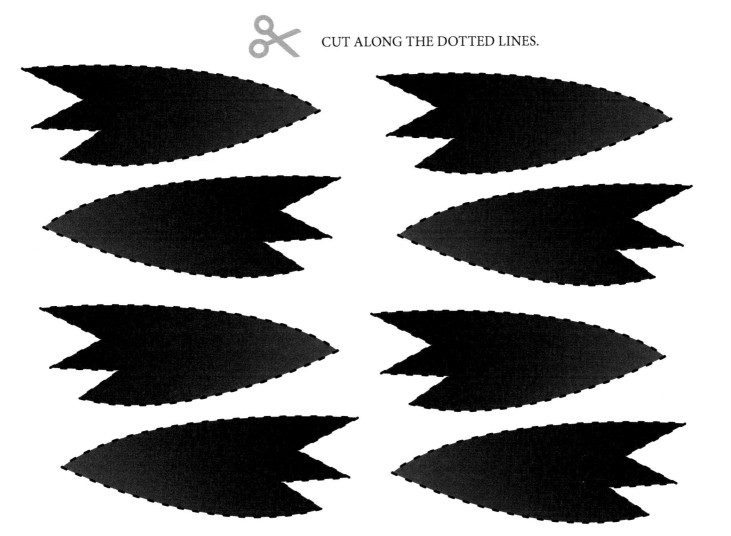

Cut out the wings and write your party guests names on the back. Stick a piece of double-stick tape on each wing. Then blindfold each guest, spin them around and play Pin-the-Wings-on-Little-Hoo! Whoever gets the wings closest to where they should go, wins!

CAN YOU FIND THESE ITEMS IN THE STORY?

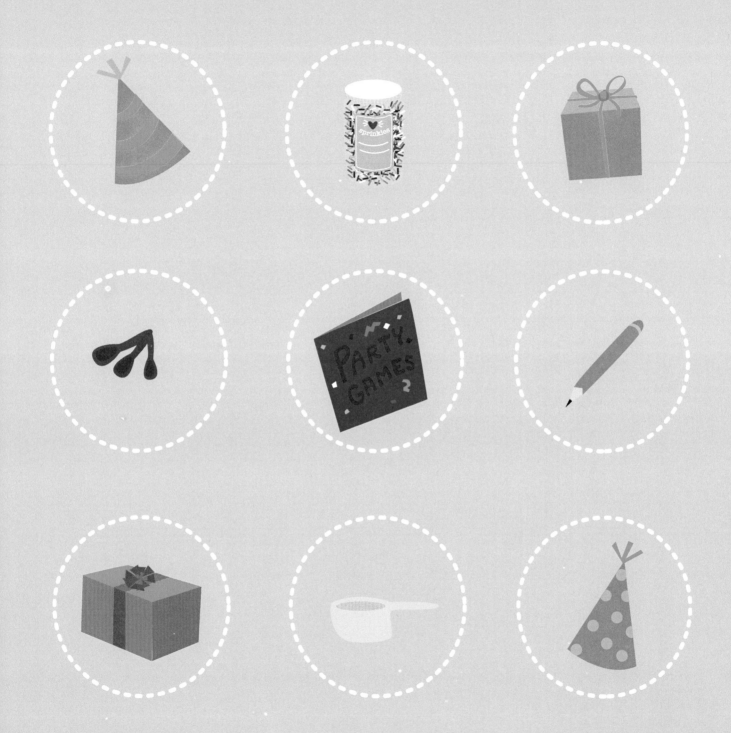

Made in the USA
San Bernardino, CA
30 September 2017